A DON BLUTH FILM

All Dogs Go To Heaven™

MOVIE NOVELIZATION

Based on the motion picture from
Goldcrest and Sullivan Bluth Studios Ireland Ltd.

Executive Producers
George A. Walker and Morris F. Sullivan

Produced by
Don Bluth * Gary Goldman * John Pomeroy

Screenplay by
David Weiss

Directed by
Don Bluth

Novelization adapted b~
An~
C~

Wa~
Mal~

D1041832

Chapter 1

A steady tap tap tap echoes through a stony tunnel, far beneath the quiet grounds of the New Orleans Dog Pound. From the darkness comes an anxious whisper. "Itchy, a few more degrees to the left!"

Itchy, a loyal dachsund armed with a tool for every occasion, strains to see in the flickering beam of his miner's cap. He continues to tap his chisel in search of his best friend's voice. "No, no, your other left!" Charlie directs his nervous buddy from behind a wall of dirt. Once a carefree hound-about-town, Charlie B. Barkin is now a mutt with a mission. Tonight, he is going to break out of this miserable prison to which he was wrongly committed.

As dogs go, dachsunds are built rather low to the ground, a fact which makes them particularly prone to getting dirt up their noses. "Ah . . . ah . . ." Itchy tries to curtail his sneeze, but it is useless. "Ah . . . CHOO!!!" Dirt and rubble fly everywhere.

"Are you gonna do that again?" asks Charlie impatiently.

"Stand back," Itchy warns as his nose gives off another tunnel shattering blast. The force of the sneeze at last clears an opening to Charlie.

"Itchy! You're a genius! Am I glad to see you,"

exclaims the convict, unable to see Itchy at all in the dark cavern. "Where are you?"

Itchy fumbles toward Charlie, smack into a steel pipe that stands between them. In his hurry to remove the obstacle, Itchy blasts the pipe with a blowtorch, which flares dangerously close to Charlie's nose. "Put that thing out!" Charlie screams. "What are you tryin' to kill me?"

"I'm sorry, boss, but the pipe . . ." Itchy explains as he produces a power drill instead.

"Wait," Charlie warns him. "I think that might be a water main."

"No, Charlie. Water mains are *green* This is *red*."

"You're color blind," Charlie reminds Itchy.

"That's true. But this is *green*."

"It's *red*," insists Charlie.

"Red?" echoes Itchy as he puts the mighty drill to work, pummeling through the water main. Water gushes from the pipe.

From the dog pound, a fountain spews forth into the night sky like an erupting volcano. Aerial search lights criss cross the pound. A siren wails. And two dogs stumble through an obstacle course of Itchy's precious tools as they hurry to escape. There is no time to stop, not even for Itchy's favorite drill. But Itchy, true to his name, can't help himself and begins scratching as bullets whizz by. Charlie yanks his pal and drags him along.

"I can't help it, Charlie. I itch when I'm nervous!" And Itchy has plenty of reason to be nervous, as the pair escapes by a tail hair from the maelstrom of searchlights and gunfire, out into the night.

Beneath a canopy of stars, crickets chirp and Louisiana bayou glistens in the moonlight. Water laps gently against a derelict freight ship, home of a floating canine nightclub, once known as "CARFACE & CHARLIE'S PLACE." That was before Carface, Charlie's greedy pitbull partner, devised a secret plot to leave Charlie in the pound, and himself in control of the entire operation. Now, on the crooked wooden sign, Charlie's name has been crossed out.

Inside, the dingy cargo room buzzes with excitement as a pack of rats careens after cheese-on-wheels, zooming around loop-the-loops along a roller coaster obstacle course of oil slicks and mattress springs toward the finish line. From his box-seat bucket, a bowtied bulldog calls the race, as dogs of every variety cheer on their lucky rat to win them a share of the club's steaks and chops.

A black and white runt named Squad Car wins the race, the long shot, leaving most of the motley crowd ripping up losing slips, downcast and broke.

"If you ask me, I think the house is rigged," complains one disgruntled fox terrier who has nothing left to bet. A luckier Chihuahua joyfully presents his winning ticket at the desk, only to be handed a moldy, half-eaten steak. He sniffs it disgustedly, not the only thing that's rotten in Carface's joint since Charlie disappeared.

But the show goes on. As a new heat begins, the dogs keep on betting and the rats keep on racing. Until suddenly, a triumphant yodel silences the hubbub. All eyes turn with shock to see, standing in the entrance of the dilapidated club, one Charlie B. Barkin.

"Whaddya know? Whaddya say?" calls the happy-go-lucky visitor. A bedraggled Itchy follows, echoing the salutation. The crowd faces them in stunned silence. Finally, a down-in-the-mouth basset hound asks what all the dogs are wondering. "Charlie, ain't you supposed to be on death row?"

"No," barks Charlie without hesitation. The dejected dogs gather round one by one, straining to believe their eyes, howling their woes to Charlie and Itchy.

"Things have changed, Charlie, since you been gone. Life hasn't been no piece of cake," explains an elderly, once beautiful Labrador.

"Carface hasn't been treating us too good," adds the hungry Chihuahua, while Charlie tests his luck at the dice table.

"Things are tough, but we carry on," the Labrador moans.

"Could you spare a couple o' bones for old time's sake?" wails the basset hound in his tattered old top hat. Charlie rolls the dice, a winning toss, and picks up his prize in bones.

"Why settle for a couple o' bones," reasons Charlie, depositing his winnings into a slot machine, "When you can have the whole bank!"

"Charlie, look! You've hit the jackpot!" And sure enough, from a huge net above, Charlie and all the gloomy onlookers are showered with choice bones and steaks.

With Charlie back, spirits begin rising again. Charlie and Itchy are the life of the party, and the nightclub alights with their song and dance. Together they howl, "You can't keep a good dog down!" with delight, crooning that no hard times or mixed up pedigree could ever hinder their success. The old gang hoists them high over their shoulders like a couple of returning heroes. Before long, everyone is singing.

All the festivity summons Killer, a mangy, nearsighted greyhound, down from the hatch to Carface's office above. At the sight of Charlie, Carface's wimpy stooge reels back in horror. How could this be? Charlie's unmistakable yodel resounds through the room. Charlie is back, *no* mistake about it!

Killer slinks back into the bright lights and gleaming automobile decor of Carface's smoky upstairs office, not anxious to inform his boss of the bad news. The gruff old pitbull is relishing a cigar in the back of his mint model T limousine, when Killer butts in to tell of Charlie's miraculous return.

"It's *him,* boss. I don't get it! I know what you're thinking, boss, but I don't know nothing about this. We set him up for good . . ."

"Killer," Carface's gravelly voice interrupts. "I do not wish to share fifty percent of the business with my partner Charlie." When he and his thugs arranged to have Charlie locked away in the pound, he was certain he would never see the mutt again. But now . . .

"You want I should go squeeze his head with the pliers?" Killer laughs evily.

"Killer. That is no way to treat an old friend," Carface explains between pitbull puffs on his foul smelling cigar. "Friends must be handled in a friendly and businesslike way." He grins knowingly at Killer, baring his shark-like teeth. He has another plan up his sleeve, intent on keeping his one hundred percent share of the profits!

Below, as the party continues, Charlie makes his way up the old familiar stairs to seek out his old partner. Carface greets him with mock surprise.

"Charlie. Oooooh," he purrs sweetly. "Is it really you?"

Charlie makes himself right at home beside an old radio, turning up the music and helping himself to one of Carface's precious candycanes. He compliments Carface on how well the business seems to be doing, but adds with a sigh of remorse, "The customers ain't laughing."

"Gamblers are never happy, Charlie."

Charlie doesn't agree, and lets Carface in on his plans for a new and improved nightclub. "This place needs some class, a little culture, and some influence from the the-a-tre. Some dancing girls . . ." He raises the volume on the radio, snapping to the music, but Carface lowers it.

"Charlie, you're right, but times have changed. You've done time, and that's no good for business! You're a dog with a record!"

"I was framed!" Charlie protests.

"I know that!" Carface sympathizes, as if he had nothing at all to do with it. He prostrates himself before his foe, crying fake tears. "You're like a brother to me and that's why . . . sniff! . . . why we need to split up the partnership!"

Charlie is shocked by the suggestion, still unsuspecting of Carface's true motives to be rid of him once and for all. His old partner convinces him, though, that he should set up his own club in a new location where nobody will know him or his criminal record, as undeserved as it may be. And to start him off, Carface generously offers Charlie half of his "stakes"—the T-bones, the porterhouse steaks, even the mignons!

But in the hidden chamber elsewhere on the boat, Itchy hears another story. During the revelry, Charlie's trusted friend accidentally discovered a secret entrance to a dingy back room. Now, from the shadows, Itchy finds himself eavesdropping on a conversation between some of Carface's goons. They argue over whose turn it is to feed "the little monster" when Killer interrupts.

"Come on, dogs," he calls, "You've got a job to do. Carface wants you should get rid of Charlie."

Itchy realizes in terror that Charlie is in trouble. He screams out desperately to warn his friend, but he cannot be heard from behind the secret panel he entered.

Back in Carface's office, Charlie shakes paws with his ex-partner. "This is sounding better all the time," he wags his tail over the deal that Itchy knows will never take place. Carface enthusiastically announces the new arrangement to his entourage of goons and directs them all to take Charlie to the Mardi Gras to celebrate, with a different plan in mind.

Chapter 2

The Mardi Gras festivities are in full force, giant floats are colorfully decorated, fireworks illuminate the sky, and crowds dance in the streets to the music that spices the night. Finally free from the secret compartment, Itchy frantically weaves his way through the noisy spectacle, dense with merry makers, to find Charlie.

Nearby, inside a deserted parade float, Carface is carrying out the finishing touches of his scheme at a send off bash for Charlie. It is a festive group, party hats and all.

"I'm sure that I speak for every dog amongst us in wishing you the best of luck in your new venture," Carface proclaims in his gravely voice. "And now, as a token of our esteem, we are presenting to you this lucky gold watch. The pocketwatch is slipped like a pendant around Charlie's neck.

Charlie is stumbling about deliriously but manages to land a sloppy lick on the watch, and amuses himself with the quip, "Takes a lickin' and keeps on tickin'!"

While the gang is singing Charlie's praises, Carface whispers the final orders into Killer's ear. "Take Charlie out back for the *big surprise*.

A panting, out of breath Itchy is closing in as Carface's goons direct a reeling Charlie to the end of the pier. Itchy is still too far away to do anything but call out Charlie's name and whimper in despair while he helplessly watches Carface's nasty plot unfold.

Killer positions a still singing Charlie on the mark at the end of the rickety wooden pier and blindfolds him. "Now stay here and don't peek, Charlie, Killer instructs before joining Carface at the other end of the pier. Carface releases the brakes on an old model car and switches into gear. Slowly, it begins rolling down the dock towards its unsuspecting victim. "Goodbye Charlie," Carface chortles. The bright headlights glare menacingly as the car is set on its deadly collision course with Charlie. Itchy desperately yells but Charlie is too slap happy to hear him, belting out the last notes of his song, when the car slams into Charlie mid-yodel, sending him flying off the pier. Dog and car crash into the water with a thunderous splash.

* * * * *

As Charlie plunges deeper and deeper into the river, bright lights and colors sparkle in fantastic display. Charlie shoots through them, like a tunnel that leads finally to a strange and wonderful place. Ethereal clouds part to reveal an ornate gateway, sparkling with diamonds and sapphires and rubies.

"Where am I?" wonders a startled Charlie.

"This is the Great Hall of Judgment," a beautiful Whippet magically appears to greet him.

"Judgment!" Charlie jumps nervously at the thought.

"Oh, not to worry Charlie. You'll go to Heaven. *All dogs go to Heaven,* because unlike people, dogs are naturally good and loyal and kind."

Charlie relaxes and agrees, "That's true." The elegant Whippet, crowned by a plume of pink hair, takes Charlie on a tour of his future home.

"This is really a lovely place you've got here," Charlie observes, floating over majestic clouds where lions and lambs lie together. The Whippet welcomes Charlie to a place that is always ordered and calm. Everything seems perfect until the Whippet points out that Charlie is dead!!! "What! You mean I'm . . . I'm . . ."

"Stone cold, I'm afraid," the Whippet assures him.

"I can't believe it. I've been murdered!" Charlie is outraged.

The Whippet studies Charlie's pages in the Great Hall of Judgment Book. "Hmmm . . . I'm having trouble finding any goodness or loyalty here, but, let's see."

Charlie can't concern himself with that. All he can think about is CARFACE! "He killed me. There's a mistake been made here." Charlie pleads his case with the beautiful dog, as he is adorned

13

with a robe, wings and a halo by passing cherubs. "My time's not up yet."

"Oh yes it is. There's no mistake about that." The Whippet tells Charlie as they float up to layers of clouds where countless clocks are ticking and chiming. "See this watch is your life and, it's stopped."

"Oh. Can't you just wind it up or something?" Charlie ponders hopefully, while sloughing off his heavenly accoutrements.

"And send you back? Oh, we musn't do that. No one's ever allowed to go back." The Whippet encourages Charlie to stamp his paw print in the Book of Records, where everything about him— past and future—is on file.

"You mean there's no surprises or anything?" remarks a disenchanted Charlie.

"Heaven is a wonderful place," the Whippet enthuses.

"No surprises," moans Charlie again before asking the Whippet to dance. Together, they waltz on a cloud as Charlie mourns the wonders of heaven.

"Everything is so lovely here. So planned. So ordinary . . . and that's what's driving me crazy." Charlie recounts all the exciting plans he still has in store. Adventure! Love! Surprises! Heaven leaves him nothing to look forward to. He longs to return to his old life, and even though he doesn't like to steal, Charlie realizes that switching the watch Carface gave him for his heavenly watch is his only chance.

The Whippet is so charmed by Charlie as they glide through the cosmos of shooting stars and cratered moons, that it is too late when she realizes that he is up to no good. "Charlie, what are you doing?" Behind his back, Charlie is rewinding his watch! "Charlie, don't wind that watch!" As the Whippet screams his name, there is an explosion of light. Charlie is catapulted back through the colored tunnel to life on Earth. The haunting voice of the Whippet echoes behind him. "You can never come back . . ."

A coughing, gasping, half drowned Charlie pulls himself out of the water and onto the pier, startling a sleeping cat. He shakes the water out of his faltering watch, which glows from its perch about his neck, echoing the Whippet's final words of warning. Charlie is having none of that. He slams the watch cover shut, and begins his painful journey through the bleak, rainy night to Itchy's ramshackle junkyard tool shed.

Surrounded by a clutter of tools and car parts, Itchy whimpers in his sleep as he relives Charlies' horrible accident in a dream. In his nightmare, Carface is now wrapping his hands around Itchy's neck to choke him. He is relieved to wake up to find that it is really only Charlie shaking him.

15

"Itchy, it's okay little buddy. It's me. Charlie."

"Charlie, it's you. I saw Carface and he was grabbing my neck," rambles a jittery Itchy only to stop mid-sentence and add quite calmly, "Oh, hi, Charlie," before shrieking as if he's seeing a ghost! Charlie tries to quiet the frightened dachshund, but Itchy is determined to get as far from the spooky apparition as fast as he can. "Oh Charlie, get away from me! Get back. Don't hurt me!" A terrified Itchy tries to bribe the ghost throwing everything from his 9-piece ratchet set to a Rolls Royce hood ornament from his prized tool chest.

"Quiet, Itchy," Charlie soothes. "I'm not a ghost. I'm not dead." Itchy is not buying this news and continues to scream as loud as he can. "Will you shut up!! Itchy. I'm alive! Look . . . look, do ghosts have fleas?" Charlie confronts Itchy with positive living proof he is a real live dog. He plucks a critter off his back and flips it onto Itchy's nose.

"Charlie . . . Charlie, it's really you, but I saw the car, and the river, and your lifeless body flying through the air," Itchy sobs.

"Itchy, what can I say," Charlie chuckles. "It wasn't my time."

Now that he has his Charlie back, Itchy can't stop hugging him and shouting for joy.

Charlie hushes him. He wants the news of his return kept quiet, figuring that if Carface thinks he's dead, it will be that much easier to get even with his double-crosser.

Itchy has no desire to go up against Carface and tries to persuade Charlie they should go far away. "We could share a nice little place in the Himalayas. They got gambling, they got races. They even got a town called Tibet, you know 'to bet.' "

Charlie's more interested in figuring out how Carface's operation got bigger without him, the brains of the outfit. "He's got something up his sleeve," Charlie thinks out loud. "Yeah, a gun!" says Itchy.

Itchy has a pretty good idea of what Carface does have and doesn't mind giving Charlie an inventory. "Carface has got thugs and they got muscles . . . knives . . . and he's got a monster in his basement . . ."

"Monster??" Charlie repeats with interest. "Hmmm, monster." Perhaps he can unravel the mystery of Carface's success. How strange . . . a monster!

Chapter 3

Itchy wants to go spying at Carface's, and on a monster no less, about as much as he'd like to go to a dog catcher's convention. He resists with every step, but Charlie prods his pal along into a secret air vent at Carface's nightclub, where the two have a hound's eye view of the boat's dungeon room. Nestled between a labyrinth of pipes is a bed, beside which stands a figure in rags.

"Charlie, I just know we're both going to die." In a situation like this, Itchy does the only sensible thing, he scratches himself like mad. Charlie has no patience for this. All he can think about is the monster.

Charlie grabs the terrified Itchy by the tail which only frightens him more. "Now *there* is your monster," Charlie chides his buddy as they peer through the vent's grating as the monster pulls back its rags, revealing a sweet little girl with short dark hair, topped by a bow. She wears a tattered, patched dress and clutches a rag doll at her side.

"Well I'll be . . ." remarks an astonished Itchy as he watches the little girl speaking gently to a caged rat.

Carface appears in a cloud of cigar smoke with Killer trailing behind. "Mr. Carface, can I go outside today?" the little girl asks politely.

"Sure you can little girl. But *first* you talk to the rat." Carface puts his head right up to the cage, not sparing the scared rat from the sickening cigar smoke. Even Killer coughs in protest.

Charlie and Itchy discover Carface's secret. This is no ordinary little girl. This little girl can talk to animals (including dogs) and they can talk to her! After a kindly pat on Mr. Longtail's head, the girl asks after the other rats that race on Carface's track. "Twizzle has a cold?" the child translates after Mr. Longtail utters a string of rat noises. "She could drink soup," the kindly child suggests.

This continues, but Carface grows impatient with the little girl's concern for the animals. "Hurry it up. Hurry it up."

"I'm sorry," the girl murmurs before getting to the one question Carface cares about. "So who do you think will win?" After a few more sounds from Mr. Longtail, the child reveals, "Oh, I see. The Spotted Grey."

Carface, armed with the information he came for, grabs the cage to leave. With this kind of inside knowledge on the rats, the conniving pitbull has a tremendous advantage over his gambling customers. "Shift the odds on the Spotted Grey and feed the kid," Carface orders.

"Oh boss, do I have to?" whines Killer.

"But Mr. Carface, you said I could go outside today." The little girl looks up sadly at the departing dogs. The door slams behind them leaving no doubt that the little girl is not going anywhere. She sits down in a corner, weeping to herself.

Up in his hiding place, Charlie is licking his chops. "A little girl who talks to animals!" It doesn't take a great thinker like Charlie long to figure out what a golden opportunity this is. His eyes are green with dollar signs. The jingle of imagined cash registers are music to his ears. "Poor child, we'll kidnap her . . uh, rescue her," Charlie informs Itchy as they make their way through the grating and down a stack of crates to the small child.

"Uh little girl . . ." Charlie softly calls for her attention. At first she is frightened, but as Charlie talks to her, she comes out warily from behind a staircase. "Excuse me. Am I to understand that you're being held here against your will? Let me introduce myself. I'm Charlie B. Barkin and this is my associate, Ichiford "Itchy" Dachshund. Mr. Itchy to you. And it strikes me that this is not the kind of place for you." Charlie offers to take the girl away, already setting to work packing her few possessions for her. He wonders aloud where her parents are.

"I'm an orphan," the girl sadly admits.

As far as Charlie is concerned that's all the better. She can stay with Itchy. "What's your name little girl?" Charlie inquires, but before she can fully answer, Itchy makes it perfectly clear that he wants out of Carface's boat and any involvement with this girl. Charlie straps the packed bag to Itchy and gallantly offers to let the girl stay with himself instead, giving her a doggy-back ride out of the basement.

"Anne Marie."

"Huh?"

"You asked my name. My name is Anne Marie," declares the girl in a spunky tone.

"Yeah, sure," Charlie goes on hardly listening to her as he lists the benefits of staying with him. "Canopy bed under the stars. Open hearth, and three square meals a day. Radio, heater, white walls. I live in a cab. Low mileage, of course . . ." To himself, Charlie is considering the high mileage Anne Marie should be able to afford him. The secret of Carface's success is now under new management!

Carface is not a happy pitbull when he learns that his golden goose has been stolen. Through clenched teeth, Carface makes himself understood *loud* and clear to Killer. "I loved that girl. I want her back. NOW!!!" Killer slinks away, not about to dispute Carface's sincerity.

* * * * *

The scene is definitely more peaceful over by the junkyard, where a full moon glistens over the line of rusted-out cars, leading to Charlie's cluttered but cozy taxi cab. All the comforts of home are here including an old Victrola which plays a soothing jazz number to fit the mood. Charlie is telling a bed time story for Anne Marie. Itchy is not impressed. Never mind that his book is upside down, or that it is a copy of *War and Peace*, Charlie B. Barkin is improvising his own version of *Robin Hood*.

"This sheriff is a real bimbo. What say we knock him off and take the gold, not for ourselves, but we'll give it to the poor suckers who got took in the first place."

"Hey boss, where do you get that stuff," Itchy grabs the book. "What kind of hood is this guy anyway, giving dough to the poor and without taking his cut?"

"I like this story Mr. Itchy."

"You would," Itchy accuses Anne Marie.

"Shut up" Charlie whispers to Itchy. "I'm trying to get the little brat to sleep." Charlie polishes off the story of Robin Hood and Maid Marian in another sentence or two and announces it's bed time. Then, tossing an old quilt over Anne Marie, he draws a curtain which separates the front and back seats.

Itchy and Charlie sit beneath the star-speckled sky outside the cab and talk a little business. Itchy is still nervous about the whole deal. With Carface looking for the girl, it's like sitting on a time bomb!

"Would you relax," Charlie calms his pal. "Carface ain't gonna look for her here. He thinks I'm dead. Remember? Now get some sleep. Tomorrow we take this little time bomb to the horse track and we make ourselves a fortune."

"Horsies?" giggles Anne Marie who is obviously not asleep, much to Charlie's dismay. Itchy and Charlie arrange to meet bright and early the next day.

Charlie hops into the back seat of the cab and tosses a pillow to Anne Marie. Just as he settles down, he hears a small voice. "Charlie, would you please tuck me in. Please?" With as good natured a smile as he can muster, Charlie briskly tucks her in. No sooner has he done this than . . . "Charlie, may I please have a good night kiss?" This request is a little harder for Charlie, but he finally musters the daring to give Anne Marie a half-hearted lick. As soon as he is back behind the curtain, he wipes off his snout and quietly voices his disgust, "Yuck!"

"Thank you for rescuing me," Anne Marie sweetly praises Charlie as he closes his eyes. An annoying chorus of squeaky springs can be heard from the front seat as Anne Marie tries to get comfortable.

"Hey Squeaker," Charlie calls to Anne Marie. "Knock it off."

"I'm sorry," Anne Marie apologizes, but in a moment, she crawls beside Charlie, unable to sleep on the front seat. A desperate Charlie trades places with her. Anything to get some sleep! Charlie finally settles down only to hear the silence broken again.

"Dear God, thank you so much for my new best friend, Charlie . . ." Charlie tries everything to ignore the prayers. ". . . And thank you for sending him to rescue me . . ." He peeks his snout through the seat curtain, annoyed. ". . . And God bless Mr. Itchy, and God bless Charlie. Amen. Oh and please help me find a mommie and daddy."

The little girl's magic has managed to infect Charlie for a moment. As she finishes her prayers, the brazen, old mutt is feeling a bit like a heel. But even so, he is relieved when all is quiet.

A sleepy Anne Marie wonders between yawns, "Charlie, do you think you could help me find a mommie and daddy?"

"Kid, I'll help you find the lost city of Atlantis. Just please, please go to sleep!"

As the moon shines over the sleepy junkyard, it seems Charlie has, at long last, gotten his silence. Almost. Anne Marie's urgent whisper pierces the night. "Charlie. I have to go to the bathroom."

Chapter 4

It is a glorious morning at the fairground. Horses can be heard whinnying inside the bright red-roofed racetrack stable. If the night before Charlie was having a hard time getting Anne Marie to go to sleep, he is having a harder time now getting her to talk to the horses.

"Maybe the horses is too stupid to talk," Itchy suggests. For stating that notion, a bay mare by the name of Stela whinnies loudly and whacks Itchy with a toss of her head which sends him reeling.

Charlie is anxious to know what the horse's neigh means. "What'd she say?"

"You sound just like Mr. Carface." Anne Marie accuses Charlie as she turns her back on him.

Charlie is moritifed to be compared to his double crossing ex-partner. "What?! He's a criminal!! Did he read you stories?! Charlie pleads, but Anne Marie avoids him. Charlie struggles to find reasons why he's not just like Carface. "Did he give you a comfortable bed? Did he kiss you goodnight? You're talkin' to Charlie here. I rescued you," With a sudden inspiration, he adds, "And besides, we're giving money to the poor."

"Boss!" Itchy, who is starting to wonder about Charlie's sanity, immediately objects.

"Sharing the money with the poor," Charlie amends his plan.

Anne Marie perks up at this. "You mean like *Robin Hood*?"

"And another thing," Charlie confides, "if you're serious about this mommie and daddy business you're gonna need a little dough of your own. You know, new dress, new shoes. I know about these things. Nobody wants a scrawny little doll in rags!"

"Promise? You'll help me find a mommie and daddy?" Anne Marie is growing excited.

"Sure. I promise."

"Oh, Charlie!" Anne Marie gives Charlie a great big hug. Any doubts she had about her best friend have vanished. Itchy is sick of the whole thing, but in her happiness, Anne Marie scoops him up into her arms as well. Isn't that wonderful?" She laughs. He growls at her. Anne Marie puts the protesting Itchy down at the sound of the Bay mare's whinny. "Excuse me," Anne Marie politely approaches the horse, "could you please tell me which one of you is going to win today's race? We're going to give the money to the poor and buy me a new dress so I can get some parents."

The stylishly groomed mare neighs her approval and tells Anne Marie that the Grand *Chaw Hee* will win because it's his birthday. Anne Marie repeats this for Itchy and Charlie. The two dogs stare at the Grand *Chaw Hee* in disbelief. The Grand *Chaw Hee* is a broken down plug horse who can't even keep the flies away. "But you mustn't tell," Anne Marie whispers. "It's a surprise."

"I'll say," Itchy mutters not truly convinced. Charlie's doubts are whinnied away by Stella and he is ready to place the bet. Of course placing a bet takes money and Charlie and Itchy have a mischevious plan to get some. They wander through the racetrack crowds.

"All we need now is a couple of bucks." Charlie figures.

"A couple of bucks, a couple of bucks." echoes Itchy.

"A couple, a couple," Anne Marie picks up the chant thoughtfully. "Hmmm, yeah, a mom and dad!"

For their pickpocketing purposes, the people Charlie and Itchy check over at first all seem too thin or too fat. Suddenly, Anne Marie, who has been looking over the crowd for parent material, shouts, "Oh look! Charlie, they're perfect!" A young, well-groomed couple stands talking with each other several yards from Anne Marie.

Charlie agrees but for quite a different reason. He and Itchy begin their plan of attack. While

Itchy distracts the couple with his lame dog routine, Charlie attempts to lift the man's wallet with his teeth. Anne Marie is oblivious to the dogs' plan and innocently rushes over to help Itchy.

"Oh, is this your dog?" The woman named Kate wonders.

"Well, kind of," Anne Marie replies. Itchy lets out a howl that startles everyone, allowing Charlie to grab the wallet, and the two dogs disappear into the crowd. Anne Marie calls after Itchy with great concern.

"Seems to be just fine," The man named Harold reassures her.

"What's your name little girl? the lady asks kindly.

"Anne Marie," she informs them coyly with a curtsy. "Pleased to meet you." Anne Marie goes on, hoping to make a good impression, but then she glances down to notice her ragged clothes. "I'm getting a new dress," she informs them.

"Oh, that's nice dear. Where are you parents?" Kate inquires obviously more concerned with that than Anne Marie's clothes.

Anne Marie is certain she is making excellent progress with the couple she has selected when her progress is cut short by an insistent whisper from behind a cluster of bushes. "Squeaker. Let's go!"

"But I want to talk to the . . ." Anne Marie starts to whisper back.

"Come on, we're gonna miss the Grand Chawhee's birthday."

And with that, Charlie plants a man's hat on her head and yanks her away.

As an announcer broadcasts the last call for bets, stragglers approach the betting windows. One of them is a man with a strange figure, and an equally strange wobble. Anne Marie, in a mustache and a hat, is balanced on Itchy's shoulders, and Itchy is balanced on top of Charlie, with the three of them covered by a long coat.

The betting information is passed up from Charlie to Itchy to Anne Marie, who places the bet in the deepest voice she can muster. "Grand Chawhee to win." The situation has Itchy in a nervous state. He is scratching away and Anne Marie must scratch him too before they all fall over. The bespectacled cashier gapes at the Grand Chawhee's terrible odds, wondering if this peculiar bettor knows something. "It's his birthday," Anne Marie declares in her regular voice, quickly covering by slipping back into her best baritone. She thanks the cashier for the ticket, and the three wobble away to the racetrack grandstand.

A trumpet blasts the pre-race fanfare. The race will begin any moment. Anne Marie is licking an ice cream cone, most of which is dripping on the two dogs inside the coat. Suddenly the starting bell rings, the gates open and the horses are off! The Grand Chawhee manages to leave his post backwards. And as if that were not enough, there is a new stallion in the race, the posh Lord Reginald, who does not know about the Grand Chawhee's birthday surprise and is doing his best to win.

It does not look good for the Grand Chawhee, but Anne Marie believes in him and cheers him on. "Come on Chawhee!! You can do it! It's your birthday!"

"Yoo hoo!" The mare Stella catches up to Reginald.

"Jolly good day for a race! Wot?" Reginald exchanges pleasantries in his clipped British accent. Stella wastes no time in telling Reginald exactly what is what in her southern drawl and the stallion's pace slows on the spot. Stella nudges the pathetic Chawhee along and sets the birthday boy into a flying leap over the finish line into a cloud of dust, much to his and everyone else's amazement.

Charlie, Itchy and Anne Marie are wild with joy. Anne Marie has a big kiss for Charlie which he wipes off with a "Yuck" when she looks back proudly at the Grand Chawhee in the winner's circle.

And so begins the trio's winning streak. They go to every kind of sporting event with animals, from frog jumping to kangaroo boxing. Anne Marie has a chat with the animals, determining the winner before each match, and the money pours in for Charlie and his pals. The winnings are piling up much to Charlie's and Itchy's delight, but there are still no parents for a downhearted Anne Marie.

Charlie is no fool, so when he notices how unhappy Anne Marie is, he takes her on a shopping spree. Itchy and Charlie yodel their approval as Anne Marie poses in outfit after outfit. The three feel on top of the world, and in a smart new blue dress, Anne Marie feels she has taken the first steps toward catching the eye of potential mommies and daddies.

At last the time has come for Charlie to set his grand scheme into motion. The plans are drawn, the junkyard cars are recycled into building material, stacked one on top of the other for the construction of Charlie's gala nightclub. Itchy and his beloved tools receive their best work out ever.

At last, the big moment has arrived and Itchy flips an electric switch. A welcome sign for CHARLIE'S PLACE lights up, and Christmas lights sparkle to the pinnacle, where colored beams alight the sky.

The regulars are all there for the opening. Lights flash and dancing girls line the stage. A red convertible serves as the bar where the old-timers gather, having more fun than ever at Carface's club. Charlie sports a party hat, and while he admires himself in a car mirror, he notices one dissatisfied customer: Anne Marie. She's dressed in her ragged old dress and holds her suitcase firmly in one hand.

"Hey. What is this? What are you doing?" Charlie asks her.

"I'm leaving," a furious Anne Marie announces. "You said we were gonna help the poor and we didn't. You promised to find me parents. You didn't even look. All you do is gamble and it isn't right."

Charlie thinks quick. If he doesn't do something to right things with Anne Marie, she is about to walk out the door. "You know something, you're right. What a selfish, callous cad of a heel I've been." Anne Marie isn't buying Charlie's act, but he doesn't give up. "Thank you for helping me to see the light! Squeaker, we're going to go out and help the poor."

Always quick to forgive her best friend, Anne Marie sighs. "Oh, Charlie," before planting a kiss on his snout. Of course when Anne Marie isn't watching, Charlie reacts with his usual "Yuck!"

Itchy has witnessed all this and is growing steadily more distressed. "Hey boss. What is it with you and this little kid? I mean. We got a business to run, you know."

Wiping off the kiss with a bar towel, Charlie explains, "Itchy, we gotta keep the little kid happy, right?

Charlie, Itchy, and Friends singing, "Can't Keep a Good Dog Down."

Anne Marie talking to animals.

Charlie learning the "do's and don'ts" of Heaven from the Whippet.

Charlie in his taxicab home reading a bedtime story to Anne Marie.

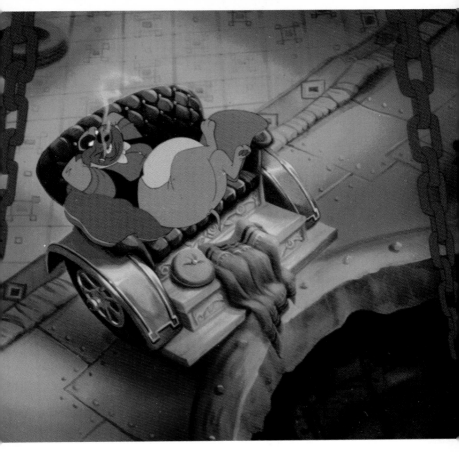

Carface planning to get Anne Marie back from Charlie.

Charlie and Itchy take Anne Marie shopping.

*Charlie and Flo watch as Anne Marie introduces
herself to the orphan puppies.*

Charlie and King Gator sing a duet.

* * * * *

News travels fast; good for some, and not so good for others.

Carface is watching as the hungry piranhas in his pit devour a hunk of meat attached to a rope the second it hits the water. The bone that is pulled back out has been stripped clean. Carface is pleased. The next in line to be sent down into the pit is Killer who is hanging upside down.

Carface is seething. He blows smoke into Killer's face as he hisses. "Charlie's alive, and I know he's got the girl. Killer, this is strike two. You're out."

"No wait boss, boss," Killer protests wildly. I get one more strike boss, honest."

Carface makes up his own rules and coldly orders his goons to lower Killer into the pit. "Nothing personal, Killer. It's business."

Killer continues to plead as he is lowered into the dark pit with the razor toothed piranhas jumping below. Carface has sadly come to realize that if he wants something done right he has to do it himself. "How to handle Charlie?" he wonders aloud. "Knives? Poison? Car didn't work. Something very special . . ."

Killer desperately screams as the piranhas snap at him, "Boss pull me up. Please. I gotta gun."

"Gun?" Carface is interested and growls, "What do you mean you have a gun?" Carface is in no hurry to pull up the hysterial Killer out of the water. "What kind of gun?" At last Carface has Killer hoisted back up till they are face to upside down face.

"A Flash Gordon Therm Atomic Ray Gun, boss."

"Ray gun!"

Billows of smoke pour from Carface's devilish grin accompanied by a most sinister laugh.

Chapter 5

A spooky cackle is heard from an old abandoned stone church surrounded by a graveyard beneath gnarled trees. "Who does his evil deeds in the shadow dark of night . . . the phantom does," . . . the disembodied voice laughs, as a strange shadow lurches up the long dilapidated rows of stairs. Then a familiar voice, huffing and puffing says, "These are some of the poorest people I know." It's Charlie and Anne Marie, and Charlie is balancing five flat boxes on top of his head. As their heads peer over the top step, they see the dozen members of Flo's puppy orphanage transfixed on a radio horror show in a time-worn room cluttered with mismatched second hand furniture. The sound of a creaking door and a loud scream from the radio sets the puppies to yapping nervously. Charlie breaks the tension by calling out, "Hey, anybody here order a pizza?"

"Charlie!" The delighted puppies greet their pal. This is soon followed by a chorus of squeals for "Pizza!" In no time, the noisy puppies are dispersing in a goo of cheese and tomatoes and olives and anchovies. Anne Marie and Charlie laugh at the messy scene.

Charlie tries to be heard above the confusion. "Hold it!" The pups look up as Charlie continues. "I want you kids to meet a very, very special guest! Anne Marie."

Still giggling a bit, the ever polite Anne Marie curtsies. "Pleased to meet you." The puppies pause for a moment to eye up the new visitor, but then dive back to attack their pizza feast.

Flo, the caretaker of these fun loving orphan pups is an elegant, fur-collared Collie. She can't help but laugh too. "Hello Charlie. It's nice of you to come by. We don't see much of you anymore."

"Well you know how it is, I mean, I've got a business to run."

One of the little pups, covered in cheese, is anxious for seconds on pizza and gets Charlie's attention by teething playfully on his leg! "Uncle Charlie," the young beagle asks, "Can I have some more?"

Charlie is only too happy to indulge the puppy and shoves a whole box at him. This sets the puppies to fighting over the pizza that is left. Uncle Charlie does his best to teach the puppies about sharing. The puppies are unwilling students at first, but then make a game of the lesson. Alas, when it is time for dessert, the puppies look like they have already forgotten about sharing as they throw themselves on the lush chocolate cake!

Away from the hubbub, Anne Marie finds a wallet on the floor by the circular stairs going up to the attic. She opens the wallet and sees a wedding photo of Kate and Harold, the couple from the race track.

"Charlie, where did you get this?"

"Well, I un . . . I uhh I . . ."

"You stole it!" Anne Marie gasps.

Charlie is ashamed. "I was gonna give it back," he lies.

"You stole it!" is all the horrified child can say. Tears well in her eyes.

"Hey Squeaker. Come on, kid." Charlie doesn't really know what to say this time. Anne Marie feels all alone and climbs the spiral stairs up to the narrow moonlit church attic without even looking back. One of the tiny girl pups, a saddened Cocker Spaniel, slowly follows her.

With her stuffed rag doll nearby, Anne Marie sits on a soft-feather blanket near a window that is illuminated by the night sky. Stars twinkle outside as she gazes at the pictures of Kate and Harold and only imagines what it would be like if she, and all the puppies in the orphanage, could be a part of their happy family. While she is day dreaming, the puppy curls up by her side.

Oh how wonderful life would be with the people in the wallet! Anne Marie can picture all the moments she would share with Kate and Harold: working, playing, going for drives, romping in the park or by the shores, saying a blessing at mealtime, reading together and being tucked in at night. It is all so beautiful and loving that a wistful Anne Marie keeps this dream locked in her heart.

There are all kinds of dreams. Daydreams and the pleasant dreams with which Anne Marie drifts off to sleep this night. And then there are dreams that are not so warming . . . bad dreams.

Charlie is also asleep at the old church. The ticking of his heavenly watch begins pulsing with the Whippet's warning, "You can never come back."

Charlie is having a nightmare visit to a very different Great Hall of Judgment. In his imagination, his watch explodes, jolting him to a place paved with dark, threatening cumulus clouds, nerve-jarring electrical currents and rockets of fire unleashed from the ground. A terrified Charlie tries to flee, but a black funnel engulfs him. As he is being sucked in, a howling Charlie is deposited into a fiery pit of red hot molten lava. A winged, black-hooded creature greets him with a fearsome grin. Charlie falls onto a small boat only to see the Evil Dog, who rules over this forsaken place of endless despair, rise from a sea of flames. Thunder and lightning boom and crackle. The fire breathing Evil Dog roars with wicked pleasure. "Now you are mine!" This Dog blasts his fiery breath at Charlie, spitting fireballs which transform into evil canine sprites that torment the helpless mutt. Charlie has nowhere to escape, sinking into the lava until at last these gruesome noises and sights are replaced by the voices of the dear little orphan pups waking him up from his worst of all possible bad dreams.

When he is finally able to shake off these terrifying images, Charlie's first thought is of Anne Marie. "Where is that kid?"

"She went to 402 Maple Street," a pink-ribboned puppy tells him, straining to remember, "to the wallet family."

At the home of Kate and Harold, Anne Marie finds all her daydreams coming to life. Kate and Harold, dressed in their night clothes, are even more wonderful in person. They were so grateful for the girl performing the good deed of returning their wallet, that they invited Anne Marie to stay for breakfast.

"You like waffles?" Kate asks as she cooks some right at the sunny kitchen table. Anne Marie has a mouth full of the delicious breakfast but manages to answer. "Oh yes, very much. Thank you."

"No. Thank you!" Harold says over his opened newspaper, thinking about the returned wallet.

"This is the most beautiful house I've ever seen," Anne Marie compliments between chews.

"Well, thank you Anne Marie. Where do you live?" Kate inquires as she serves Anne Marie another waffle and pours syrup over it.

"I live with Charlie," Anne Marie explains as her eyes grow wide watching the thick syrup cover the waffle. "He's my dog."

"Ahhh!" Kate exclaims. "But what about your parents?"

"I don't have any parents."

"Then where do you stay?" Harold wonders, becoming more concerned.

"With Charlie in the junkyard," Anne Marie says matter-of-factly taking another mouthful of food.

"Oh my," Kate murmurs to herself. "Anne Marie, you sit right there." Kate motions for Harold to come with her as she gets up from the table. "Honey, come with me." The worried couple stand outside the kitchen trying to figure out what to do.

Anne Marie can see them from the breakfast table but is distracted by a loud "Psssst!" She opens one of the bay windows to the garden outside and hears another "Pssst!" from down in a bed of daisies.

"Oh, Charlie," Anne Marie gushes. "Harold and Kate are really wonderful. They weren't upset about the wallet. They gave me real waffles with butter and syrup."

"Really," Charlie chuckles nervously. "That's great. I'm glad to see you found a home for yourself."

"Do you think so?" Anne Marie asks hopefully.

"Sure. In fact I just came over to say good-bye."

"Good-bye?"

Charlie realizes that Kate and Harold are stiff competition for him, so he really lays it on. "Well, I guess you won't be needing me any more."

"Maybe you could stay too," Anne Marie suggests to a dejected looking Charlie.

"No. No. I couldn't stay. I don't want to spoil it for you. They don't want a dirty old dog like me in a nice clean home like this." Charlie looks at Anne Marie trying to appear as pathetic as possible.

"But Charlie!" Anne Marie protests.

"Don't worry about me," Charlie insists, although that is exactly what he wants. "I'll make out somehow," he adds, his voice fading. He hacks out a worrisome whopping cough. "By the way, you were one of the best friends I ever had." He coughs out the final zinger. "Enjoy your waffles."

"Charlie. Charlie wait!" Anne Marie desperately calls after him, climbing out the open window. Anne Marie could never desert her best friend. Not even for her dream.

*****

Carface and his thugs have been tailing Charlie. And now they are following him and Anne Marie as the two stroll through the fruit displays of an open-air French market, without a care in the world. They will soon be feeling otherwise. Carface, dressed today in an army helmet, has Charlie in the sights of Killer's ray gun!

"All right! A little more to the left," Carface orders Killer, who is balancing the gun. "I don't want to hit the girl. Steady. Steady. Hold it," when Charlie is centered in the gun's sights, Carface sneers and gleefully bids farewell. "Good-bye Charlie." Bursts of lights explode around Charlie as he is zapped by the Flash Gordon Thermal Atomic Ray Gun.

"Oh no! Charlie!" cried a shocked Anne Marie as the ray gun blasts her pal and demolishes the barrels of apples behind him.

"Got him!" crows a satisfied Carface.

Anne Marie shakes Charlie, terrified, calling his name. Slightly dazed but still alive, Charlie clasps his heavenly watch which is merely nicked and exclaims, "Whew! You beautiful little ticket!" But there is not a moment to lose. The two have to move fast to escape from the menacing gang. "Come on. We've got to get out of here," Charlie urges as he scoops Anne Marie onto his back and runs.

"He's getting away!" Carface barks. "Fire!" Killer fires, but the weapon shoots out of control, pureeing the fruit and vegetables in the displays and anything else in its way. Killer can't turn the ray blasts off, leaving Carface and his goons scrambling and dancing to avoid being hit. "I'm surrounded by morons!" Carface rages as Charlie and Anne Marie disappear over the vegetable stalls and duck into a warehouse.

Charlie and Anne Marie hide in a broken down

wooden theater storehouse that is crammed with stage props and costumes. When it seems the coast is clear, they surface, each decked out in a bit of colorful finery.

"You okay Squeaker?" asks Charlie, wearing a fire hydrant over his head and draped in strings of pearls. Anne Marie emerges topped in a plumed Peter Pan hat.

"OH Charlie, I thought they shot you."

"So did I. But Mr. Carface doesn't know who he's dealing with. I got a power of my own and I'm gonna take care of him right now!" Charlie paces across the rickety floorboards. "And there ain't nothing' or nobody that's gonna stop me." Charlie snaps his jaws to show he means business. The floorboards creak and groan worse than ever, starting to shake apart beneath his weight. "Uh ho. Walk softly Kid," Charlie warns Anne Marie as she steps near him. Not softly enough.

The floorboards give away with a crash. As they plummet into the hole, along with a trail of theatre props, Anne Marie's and Charlie's screams echo a long way down.

They land with a splash in the darkness below. Only an occasional drip of water punctuates the silence in this underground swamp, surrounded by moss-covered rafters and rubble accumulated over the years.

"My watch. Where's my watch!" Charlie calls

frantically, realizing he lost it during the fall. Anne Marie, who is developing a cough, is more concerned about where they are. "I don't know, but we've got to find that watch." A terrified Charlie starts splashing about in the ankle deep water as he desperately searches. Racing around hysterically until he hears the comforting ticking at last, the ticking suddenly stops. "Good-bye Anne Marie," Charlie sighs. He is reconciled to his fate and lies down in the water.

"Charlie, where are you going! Charlie!" Anne Marie shakes him.

Now there is the sound of multiple ticking. This has Charlie confused. "There it is," Charlie exclaims as he sees his watch bouncing along in the water as it is carried off by an unseen power. "What's going on here?"

"CHARLIE!!!!" screams Anne Marie as the two are levitated away in the same manner as Charlie's precious watch, into the pitch black shadows of the swamp.

When they can see again, the two find themselves prisoners of a tribe of chanting, drum pounding pygmy rats, dressed in a superstitious garb of teeth and bones. Hundreds of tiny torches are aflame in the eerie underground cavern. Charlie and Anne Marie are locked in rattan cages which swing from a long rope.

The rhythmic chanting and grunting grow stronger. Something is going to happen. As his cage is moved along, Charlie, with great effort, just manages to grab his watch before the cage is dropped over the ledge of the village onto a shore heaped with bones from past sacrifices.

Much to his dismay, the thud from the fall causes Charlie and his watch to be separated yet again. The pink and purple pygmy rats stand at the edge of the high wooden platform to wait and watch. A gong is sounded. It reverberates ominously.

A pair of massive bamboo gates open in the water. A huge figure can be seen just under the surface of the water honing in on Charlie and Anne Marie like an enemy submarine.

"Charlie. What's moving in the water?"

"I don't know." Charlie's voice is quivering as he sees a gigantic reptilian tail snaking around. When the biggest alligator imaginable rises onto the beach, Charlie resigns, "Squeaker. We're gonna die."

The ground shakes as King Gator trounces toward his victims with massive, jewel ringed feet. He wears a bone through his nose, a festive necklace of feathers and a tiny can for a hat. The monstrous reptile grunts contentedly with every booming step.

Ignoring Charlie's plea for his watch, he trods right over it.

Chapter 6

King Gator stalks right up to the cage. "Ah! You look like a tasty New Orleans Canine Gumbo!" croons the alligator in his deep bass drawl. He looks Charlie over as if he were a three course meal.

"No! Don't eat him. Please!" begs Anne Marie as King Gator pops Charlie into his toothy mouth, cage and all. Charlie howls his final yodel, with everything he's got.

"Ahhh!" King Gator is enchanted by his dinner's dulcet tones, and takes Charlie back out of his mouth. "How could you expect me to eat a voice as sumptuous as this?"

Charlie can't hang the watch back around his neck fast enough. King Gator continues to sing praises of Charlie's voice, so thrilled by it that he smashes his massive tail on the ground. The earth shakes and sent Anne Marie's cage flying into the water, freeing her. "Oh what do you call that voice little fella? That a baritone or a tenor?" King Gator doesn't really care as long as they can make music together. Ah, sweet harmony!!

The alligator transforms the cavern with his singing into a sparkling, colorful Hollywood musical set and together, the duo declare they will always be musical brothers. "This is for you mama!" the hip gator calls to Anne Marie as he and Charlie pass her, but Charlie notices his little friend is looking rather pale.

"You okay Squeaker?"

At first Anne Marie can only cough, but then she murmers, "Charlie. I don't feel good."

As King Gator belts out a big finish to the song, Charlie and Anne Marie are safely escorted out from this underground passage on the belly of their musical friend.

* * * * *

While Anne Marie and Charlie have escaped one close call after another, Itchy is about to have his own close encounter of the worst kind. Itchy has been managing the booming business at Charlie's place while Charlie is away. After another busy night, he is cleaning up the bar and calls to Rocky, "Relieve Jocko on guard duty. I need some help in here. Rocky?. . . Rocky?" With every unanswered call, Itchy becomes more concerned. "Rocky! Jocko?" But the answer that greets Itchy is the looming hulk of Carface climbing over the counter, sneering at him.

"Where's the girl?" Carface demands of a shuddering Itchy.

"I don't know."

"I think you do. What do you think, boys," Carface seeks opinions from his thugs, who now gather around the car-turned-bar in which Itchy is trapped.

"Please don't do this," Itchy pleads. Carface is holding him around the neck. "Oh Charlie," Itchy wimpers, feebly wishing his pal were there. "Oh no. This is a very bad idea."

"To Charlie with love," Carface proclaims, then flicks open his razor sharp claws to engrave the message. Itchy squirms around as best he can to avoid becoming a living telegram.

* * * * *

The situation has grown worse for Anne Marie's health. She is very sick and Charlie has taken her to Flo at the abandoned church on the chance she can help.

"She's burning up with fever, Charlie. She could have pneumonia," Flo worries as Anne Marie moans.

"You think she needs a vet?"

"Charlie. She's a little girl. She needs a doctor."

"A doctor? I don't know any doctors." Charlie is worried, too, and he longs to do anything he can to help Anne Marie. "I'll find one."

From downstairs a battered Itchy hollers weakly in search of his friend. "Charlie. Charlie. You here?"

"Hey. Be quiet. Little Squeaker's sick and needs her sleep."

"Oh. You're breaking my heart," Itchy limps along. "Maybe you want I should go upstairs and kiss her goodnight?"

Then Charlie notice's his friend's condition. "Itch. What happened to you?"

"What happened to me? You want to know what happened to me?" He continues angrily. "Carface happened to me with about fifty of his thugs." Itchy painfully makes his way up the stairs to Charlie.

"That dirty rat. I'm sorry Itch. I really am sorry."

"Well look what else happened while you were side-tracked." Itchy directs Charlie to look out a broken arched window. "See that!" The two gaze at the dense plumes of smoke filling the sky from the burning ruins of Charlie's nightclub. "That's our place. You were gonna fix Carface? Well, well he fixed us."

Charlie stares in silence as his dreams explode into flames. Itchy can't take any more. All the grievances that he has kept to himself since Charlie's return now come pouring out. "See boss? it's gone too far. You wanted revenge on Carface and I said 'no, please let's get out of town' but I stayed because you're my friend. And then you wanted to kidnap the girl, and I said, 'this is crazy,' but I helped ya anyway. And then we gotta dress the girl and read her stories, and she wants that we should feed the poor, and the whole while

I'm thinkin' this is stupid. She's gonna get us killed, but I stay because . . . I'm your friend. But tonight," Itchy breaks down tearfully, "tonight Charlie, he tried to kill me! And you was out gallivanting with this girl! I say we should lose the girl, get out of town Charlie, you and me, and call it even."

Charlie sympathizes with his friend but he still wants to destroy Carface and his empire. "Ah Itchy. Now the casino's gone we gotta start all over. We need the girl more than ever . . ."

Itchy is close to tears when he interrupts. "No boss, you're crazy! It's not business any more. It's personal!!!"

"Ah come on Itchy. Sure it's just business."

"You're in love with the girl! You've gone soft. You care about her!"

All this yelling has awakened Anne Marie who is slowly descending the stairs from the attic.

Charlie will say anything to keep Itchy on his side and so the last thing he would admit are his feelings for Anne Marie. So determined he is not to show how much he cares that Charlie raises his voice to protest what Itchy jealously knows is true. "I don't care about that girl. Yeah, I tell her things now and then. I even pretend to be her best friend, but it's baloney."

"I thought I was your best friend," Itchy points out hoping for Charlie to agree.

"You are my best friend," Charlie shouts. With her it's just business. It's always been business. I'm using the girl, and when we're done with her, we'll dump her in an orphanage. Is that okay with you?"

Itchy didn't mean for it to go this far. "Sure boss," he says meekly. "Anything you say . . . Oh!" Itchy realizes Anne Marie has been standing behind them, clutching her rag doll, listening the whole time. She has overhead everything!

The tears in her eyes give way to sobs. "You're not my friend. You're a bad dog."

"Squeaker . . ." Charlie is horrified and hangs his head in shame. He calls after her to explain, but this time Anne Marie isn't waiting around for anymore of his stories. She has been betrayed. "Anne Marie! Squeaker!" he calls as she walks briskly down the stone steps and out of the dark church into the rainy night. Charlie follows her, running through the graveyard searching frantically. He spots Anne Marie's stuffed toy just as it is set aglow by a flash of lightning. In that instant, Anne Marie screams, "Carface!" Charlie realizes that his foe must have gotten his paws on Anne Marie now. Charlie, his heart pounding, rushes off in the direction of the scream, still calling her name.

Chapter 7

By now, Itchy, who has been following as fast as his injuries will allow, and Flo, who came running as soon as she heard Anne Marie's scream both arrive at the little stuffed toy.

Out of breath and upset at the terrible turn of events, Flo instructs Itchy, "Take this to 402 Maple Street. She has friends there and they'll know what to do. And hurry!"

Without hesitating, Itchy grabs the ragdoll gingerly between his teeth and sloshes through the slippery rain drenched streets of New Orleans. He climbs up a heap of old furniture to bark outside one of the elegant old manor houses. An old mustachioed Terrier emerges onto one of the ornately wrought iron balconies.

"What's at 402 Maple Street?" the terrier asks curiously.

Itchy is out of breath, with no time for long stories. "Would you just tell me where it is?! Please. Charlie's in trouble and there's a little girl real sick."

The Terrier gives Itchy the directions. "What was that all about?" asks a frumpy Great Dane aroused by the din.

"Charlie's in trouble and a little girl may die," the Terrier tells him. Both dogs now bark out this urgent news, and soon more dogs are barking, passing the word along. Soon, all across the rain drenched city come the echoed howls of a dog telephone chain.

Charlie has followed Anne Marie's scent to Carface's Place. The storm racked river is washing up against the boat in large, crashing waves.

Inside, Charlie finds the cage over a wide-mouthed anchor shaft to the bayou below where Anne Marie is now being imprisoned, suspended. Charlie climbs up onto a stack of wobbling crates and looks in at his friend who is cold, wet, and shivering with fever.

"Anne Marie . . . . Anne Marie," Charlie whispers as loud as he dares. "Come on Squeaker. Wake up. I'm gonna get you out of here."

A moan and a cough are all that the little girl can manage from her tiny bed in the cage.

"You really are sick aren't you," Charlie says as he jumps down into the cage. "Just hold on kiddo. I'm gonna take you back to the Wallet family."

As Charlie is lifting the sick child into his arms, an all too familiar, and all too unpleasant laugh, is heard. "Isn't this just the sweetest thing," Carface remarks sarcastically to his thugs who are peering down at Charlie. "Take him boys," Carface barks to his ferocious gang who are only too happy to follow this order. Growling dogs pounce on Charlie from all directions. He fights them bravely, spurred on by his desire to help Anne Marie.

* * * * *

Others are trying to save the little girl, too. A loud commotion of yipping and barking awakens Kate and Harold. The sleepy couple walk downstairs. Harold opens the door just enough to get a look at what is making such a racket in the middle of the night. "What is it dear?" Kate yawns.

"Dogs," Harold tells her rather surprised. He opens the door a crack for another look. The front porch is filled with barking dogs of all sizes and breeds. Itchy demonstrates the ragdoll to Harold, who is too flabbergasted to notice. As the robed owner of the house moves to shut the door, Itchy spots his chance and slips through a small opening into the house and right through Harold's legs.

Once inside, Itchy goes up the steps getting the ragdoll exhaustedly before Kate, who is becoming more and more alarmed. "Harold. Harold, d . . . d . . . do something," Kate stutters nervously.

Charlie is still fighting gamely against Carface's goons. Two burly dobermans grab hold of a struggling Charlie and tie him with twine to the boat's massive anchor. In his efforts to break loose, Charlie kicks away an attacking wolfhound, who retaliates by chomping down with razor teeth as hard as he can on Charlie's toes. The only possible response from Charlie is one tremendous howl of PAIN!

There is only one dog in all the world who can howl like that! From the depths of his watery empire, King Gator hears his friend's musical strains bellow across the stormy night and surfaces to find its source.

The anchor Charlie is strapped to is being lowered towards the waves below its final destination. Around Charlie's neck, the heavenly watch is ticking louder and louder with the growing danger.

"Heh, heh, heh," Carface laughs. "So you see Charlie, the story has a happy ending." The anchor slows before its final plunge into the river so Carface can explain himself, perched on a pier that faces his adversary. "I keep the girl and make a fortune and you, you get to go to heaven." Carface shoves a sticky candy cane in Charlie's mouth so Charlie can only offer a muffled protest. The anchor is sinking into the water. "You don't want to go to heaven, Charlie?" Carface taunts his victim. Up to his neck in the river now, Charlie uses the end of the candy to hook his heavenly watch in order to protect it above the water. If he lets the timepiece fill with water, Charlie knows it may stop ticking forever.

Suddenly a thunderous crash has all the dogs

looking up in alarm. King Gator explodes through one side of the ship and out the other, splintering and uprooting anything that stands in his wake; a panicky voice screams, "Abandon ship!" "Let's get out of here," cries another.

Carface and Killer watch as King Gator zooms underwater to rescue Charlie, who is by now totally immersed, watch and all.

With a well-placed snap of his mighty jaws, King Gator releases the musical hound, who makes for the surface before his watch stops. The sight of Charlie scrambling onto the pier, alive, is too much for Carface. The fuming pitbull cannot find words that adequately express his rage. He is left standing there, eyes bulging, uttering shouts of frustration.

* * * * *

Meanwhile, Kate and Harold, along with Itchy, and it seems every dog in town are racing down the city roads on their way to the waterfront. There, Charlie and Carface engage in a wrestling battle while King Gator continues to assault the ship like an out of control torpedo. As the vessel rocks, the rope holding Anne Marie's cage snaps, dropping the girl into the raging river. Charlie sees this in horror, abandoning his fight with Carface. "Anne Marie!" As he makes his way towards her, the ship, fatally damaged, rolls over. Oil barrels topple and spill into the water, where sparks from an electric generator set the water surface ablaze. "Anne Marie!" Charlie calls frantically as he spots his human friend lying unconscious on a small crate, ringed by a sea of flames.

Charlie hangs his watch on a hook for safe keeping before he attempts a dangerous dive into the waters far below to save her. From behind, with a blood curdling growl, Carface leaps upon Charlie's back and sinks his teeth into his neck. Charlie screams in agony and snatches his watch back, only to drop it. Luckily, it lands on a small crate bobbing above the bayou's surface, sending it plummeting toward the fiery water below.

King Gator rams the ship again, tossing both Charlie and Carface off their ledge high above the burning waters. Carface barely manages to hang onto Charlie. The pitbull loses his grip, slips from Charlie's back, and free falls. Carface doesn't have long to tread water below.

King Gator sizes him up and delivers his culinary evaluation of Carface: "Delicious!" before swimming after the petrified dog.

Charlie readies himself and dives into the water. He paddles over to a piece of floating wood and recovers his watch. But with a quick glance over his shoulder, he realizes he hasn't a moment to spare. Anne Marie slips from the bobbing crate into the water.

"Anne Marie!" Charlie calls above the orange waters. Charlie places his watch on the crate before plunging after her. He gathers up Anne Marie and starts to bring her to the surface.

Above, a fiery log falls onto the crate, upsetting Charlie's watch which sinks into the water. While grabbing for the watch, Charlie loses his hold on Anne Marie. In clutching her again, the watch slips away. Charlie grimaces in frustration. He has to get that watch! When he reaches after it again, he almost drops the girl. Charlie looks at Anne Marie's sweet face and knows what he must do. Holding her, he swims to the surface. His watch meanwhile sinks to the muddy bottom of the river where it lands with a thud and bangs open.

Charlie and Anne Marie come shooting up out of the water coughing and gasping for air through a hole in the bottom of the boat. Fires are still blazing all around them. Charlie gently lifts Anne Marie onto a panel of driftwood floating inside the boat and gives it a mighty shove along a safe path through a hold in the ship's hull. "You can make it! You can make it kid," Charlie calls after her with as much hope as confidence. And she does. Anne Marie, atop the board flows out of the ship on the water current spilling through King Gator's wreckage.

Charlie sees that she is safely through and can now go after his watch. But already, his body is beginning to twitch and contort to the abuse his watch is taking on the river bottom. Charlie dives down to find it, but the casing inside the watch, housing the wheels and cogs that make it work, is filling steadily with water! The ticking of the watch starts to slow until the gears have totally drowned. The ticking sputters to a stop.

The wreck of a boat that was once Carface and Charlie's Place is finished off by a final magnificent explosion that lights up the night, slipping finally beneath the churning sea.

Itchy and his troop of dogs arrive in time to see the smoking remains of the ship disappear. Itchy and Flo paddle out a ways into the water looking out over the wreckage. Itchy simply says, "Charlie," as if in his heart, he knows what has happened.

The sea is calming. Out from a smoky mist appears a raft being slowly pushed to the shore by Killer. Anne Marie, unable to stop coughing, lies weakly on her stomach, police officers warn people to stand back as the red lights of the patrol cars flash rhythmically. Kate and Harold are waiting with the dogs and gasp in alarm when they catch sight of Anne Marie as her raft floats into the rays of the search lights. Ambulance attendants rush to shore with a stretcher, waiting to tend to the sick little girl.

This long night is almost over. The storm has passed. A full moon rests peacefully behind the Victorian house at 402 Maple Street, where lights still burn in the windows while the rest of the city sleeps.

Itchy limps into the spacious bedroom at Kate and Harold's house where Anne Marie is asleep under a pink quilt, her head nestled on a fluffy white pillow. Exhausted, Itchy jumps onto the bed and curls up next to the little girl.

The latch of the window clicks open. The curtains billow from a gust of wind and a few stray leaves flutter into the room. An eerie red glow overtakes the gabled rooftops outside, rising up into the shape of the Evil Dog, his evil light swirling around and around until it seeps into the bedroom and engulfs the room and the canopied bed. From out of this fiery mist, the figure of Charlie materializes, and he jumps down by the side of the bed where his two friends are sleeping.

"Oh Squeaker," whispers Charlie as he lays his head on his paws. "I'm sorry. I'm so very sorry." Anne Marie continues to sleep. From the red glare the Evil Dog calls Charlie's name in a haunting roar that knows no mercy. But what comes in response to the Evil Dog's call is a glowing blue sphere of sparking lights. This glittering presence confronts the force of despair and gloom. Suddenly, the image of the Demon explodes. The harsh red gives way to a gentle blue glow, that sparkles across the city and into the bedroom where Anne Marie sleeps.

The room is bathed in the soothing aura of the twinkling lights. Now a very different voice calls to Charlie. It is filled with peace. "Charlie. Charlie. You can come home now."

"You said I . . ." An astonished Charlie starts to speak as he recognizes the voice of the Whippet from the Great Hall of Judgment.

"Charlie. You gave your life for her. Come home."

"But what about Anne Marie?"

"Say good-bye Charlie."

Charlie is overcome with emotion. He has so much to say to Anne Marie. There is so much in his heart he has never told her. Slowly he reaches out a paw to her and then jumps on the bed. He gazes at her not knowing where to begin. Anne Marie yawns and her eyes open. Her eyes widen in joy at seeing her friend. "Charlie." Anne Marie is sleepy but pleased.

"Yeah, It's me. How you feeling kid?"

"Okay. How are you?"

"I've come to say good-bye," Charlie tells her, doing his best to be strong.

"Where are you going?"

"Just on a little trip. Listen Squeaker, I want you to do somethin' for me, alright?"

"Uh, huh," Anne Marie nods against her pillows.

"I want you to take care of Itchy, you know just while I'm gone. You got a home now and he doesn't have anybody." Anne Marie reaches out to hug Itchy and Charlie knows his little pal will be okay.

"Don't worry Charlie. I will."

"Great." Charlie clears his throat not quite knowing what to do next; then he pats the sleeping Itchy and bids him farewell. "Good-bye little buddy."

Anne Marie throws her arms around Charlie and with a lump in her throat says, "Oh Charlie, I'll miss you." She kisses Charlie on the tip of his nose. Charlie nervously clears his throat again, but does not wipe away this last kiss from Anne Marie.

"I'll miss you too Squeaker. Now you go to sleep."

Anne Marie settles back into bed. "Charlie, will I ever see you again?"

Charlie, his eyes filled with tears and the reflected image of Anne Marie, puts on a brave front. "Sure you will kid. You know that good-byes aren't forever."

"Then good-bye, Charlie," Anne Marie says having complete faith in the best friend she's every had. She pats him tenderly, "I love you."

These words touch Charlie and swept by emotion, he can barely reply. He steadies himself and nuzzling his face as close as he can to Anne Marie's whispers, "I love you too." Having finally admitted this, Charlie can hardly bear to leave the girl, but when she yawns, he reluctantly pulls himself away.

The comforting light has been waiting patiently for him, now leads him to the open window, and fades into the distance. Charlie turns his head for one last look at Anne Marie. A cascade of glistening orange light fills the sky. "Charlie, come home," the Whippet gently calls to him. Charlie leaps into the growing brightness.

Against a sparkling mauve firmament, Charlie is once again floating contentedly on his own private pink cloud near the Whippet on hers. Almost contentedly, that is. The Heavenly choir is just a bit too tame for Charlie's taste. "Hold it! Hold it! I know we're dead up here, but so's the music! Come on. Heat it up a little bit." The choir follows Charlie's suggestion and soon the place is jumping! Charlie B. Barkin is a dog with pizzaz wherever he is.

A familiar, gravely voice creates an ugly disturbance. "Yaaaa!!!! I'll get that 'gator if it's the last thing I do," roars a hopping mad Carface as he rips off his heavenly wings and robe at the entrance to the Great Hall of Judgment.

"Touch that clock and you can never come back," warns the Whippet still enclosed in a bubble of light.

"Shut up," Carface mouths off already busy tampering with his heavenly timepiece.

Putting aside her polite attempts to reason with Carface, the Whippet trails him with all the fury she can muster yells, "I SAID TOUCH THAT WATCH AND YOU CAN NEVER COME BACK!!!!"

A happier and wiser Charlie adds with a knowing wink, "He'll be back."